Little Nelly's
Big Book
(of Knowledge)

For my own beloved Mouse,
who isn't one
P.G.

For my beautiful daughter Alice,
who is also not a mouse
A.R.

Bloomsbury Publishing, London, Berlin, New York and Sydney

First published in Great Britain in January 2012 by Bloomsbury Publishing Plc
50 Bedford Square, London, WC1B 3DP

Text copyright © Pippa Goodhart 2012
Illustrations copyright © Andy Rowland 2012
The moral rights of the author and illustrator have been asserted

A CIP catalogue record for this book is available from the British Library

ISBN 978 1 4088 1845 9

1 3 5 7 9 10 8 6 4 2

Printed in China by C & C Offset Printing Co Ltd, Shenzhen, Guangdong

FSC
www.fsc.org
MIX
Paper from
responsible sources
FSC® C008047

Little Nelly's
Big Book
(of Knowledge)

Pippa
Goodhart

ILLUSTRATED BY
Andy Rowland

BLOOMSBURY

LONDON BERLIN NEW YORK SYDNEY

Little Nelly looked in a book,
and found out . . .

. . . that she was **a mouse.**

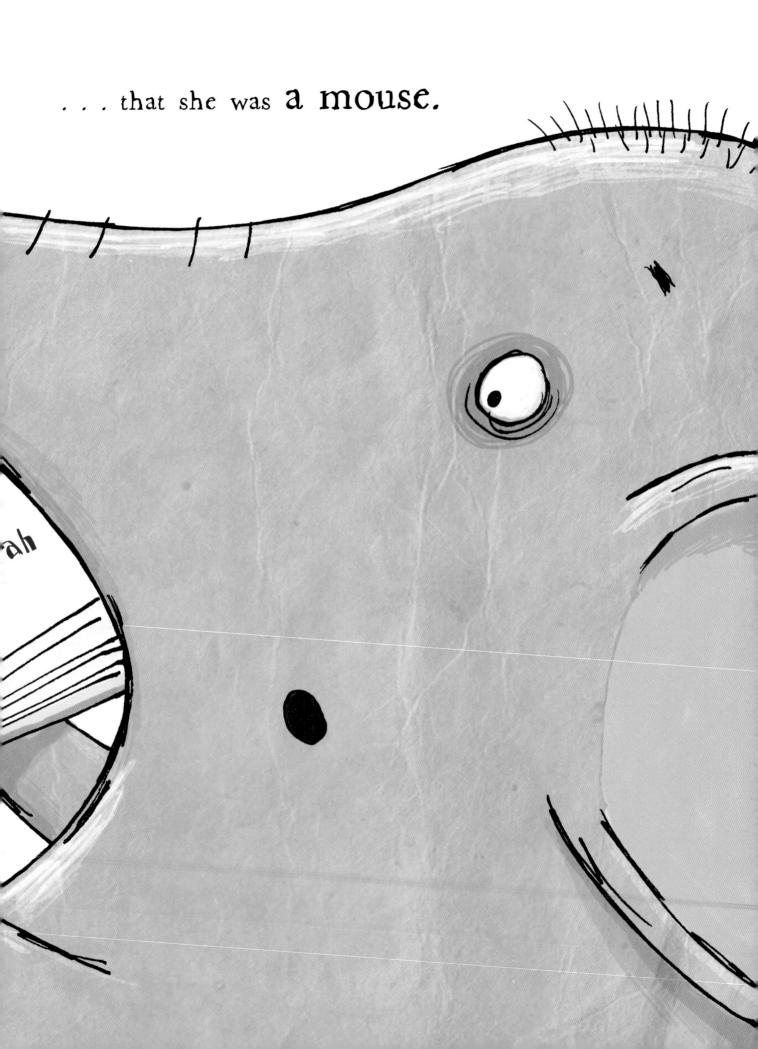

After all that reading, Little Nelly was tired.

'I need somewhere to sleep.'

Little Nelly looked
in the book again,
and she read . . .

blah

ah blah

rah blah

blah blah

ah blah blah

Mice have homes
behind holes in
skirting boards.
They like to
chew

So Little Nelly went home.

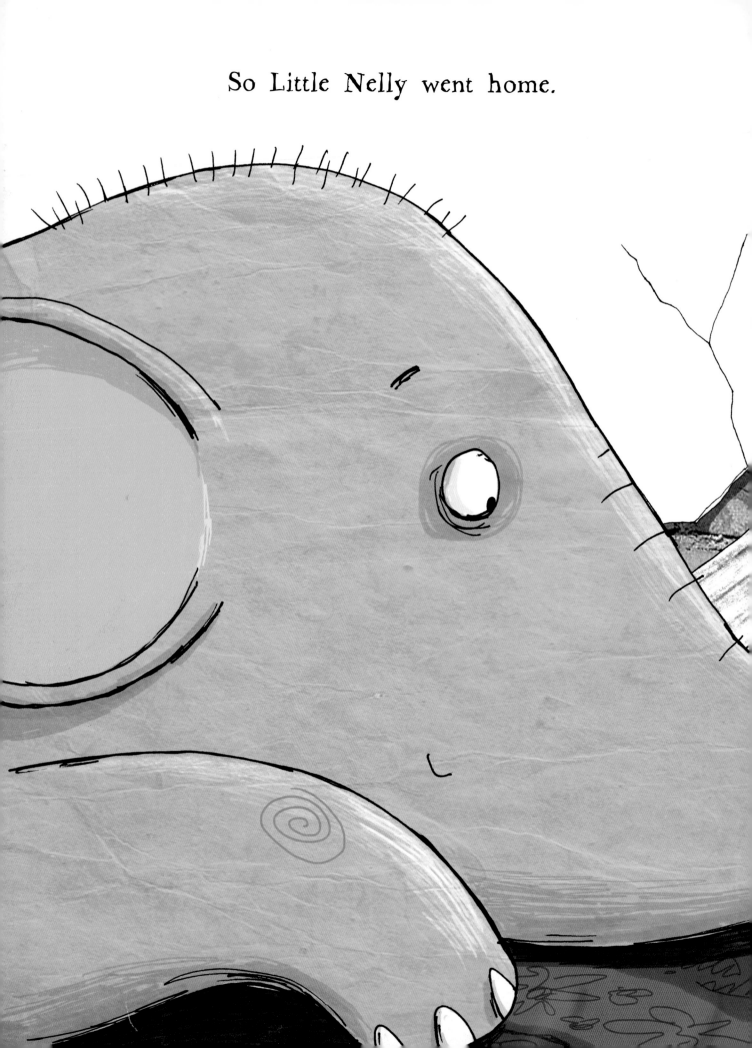

'Hello,' said Little
Nelly. 'I'm a new
mouse for your house.'

'Er, you're rather a
big mouse,' said Micky.

'I'm not!' said Little Nelly.
'If I'm a **big** mouse, why am I
called *Little* Nelly?'

'I don't think you're a
mouse at all,' said Micky.

'I am!' said Little Nelly.

'I AM! I looked in a book, and it says that I am.'

'Never mind what anybody says, Little Nelly,' said Granny Mouse. 'You're very welcome here. We'll look after you.'

And they did.

Little Nelly fitted in very well.

But even though
the other mice
were kind to her,

Little Nelly
sometimes
felt she was
different
somehow.

And she did get terribly hungry.

Granny Mouse saw how things were, and she had an idea.

'Little Nelly, I've been asking around, and I've found out that there are some other mice who are rather like you. Most of them live far away, but some live in a zoo nearby.'

'Really?' said Little
Nelly. 'Can we go
and see them, please?'

'Of course,' said
Granny Mouse.

Big
Book
OF

They all set off for the zoo.

'**WOW!** Look at them!' said Micky. 'They're just like you, Little Nelly, only these zoo mice are even bigger!'

MICE

'I told you that I'm little!' said Little Nelly.

MICE S

The zoo mice were kind and nice to the visiting mice. There were big helpings of food (and other stuff).

'Would you like to live here with us?'
asked the zoo mice.

'Yes, please!' said Little Nelly. 'We can
all be zoo mice!'

Just then, Micky came running.

'Look, Little Nelly! Look what I've found out from your book!'

'What is it?' asked Little Nelly.

'I've found out that I'm not a mouse after all!' said Micky.

'Really? Then what are you?'

'I'm **an elephant!**' said Micky.

Elephants can be:
brown
grey ✓

Elephants have
big ears ✓

Elephants have
skinny tails ✓

'That's interesting,' said Little Nelly. 'But, Micky, even though you aren't a mouse like me, I'll still be your friend.'

'Thanks, Little Nelly!' said Micky.

Which just goes to show why books
should **always** have pictures.